Norse, o: Building of the Wall

NORHALLA

Author: N.K. Stoner

Author:
N.K. Stoner

Illustrated by:
Kristin Stoner

Graphic Editor,
Layout and Design:
Samantha Stoner

Norse are the people
In stories of old
Sagas and Eddas
Their history unfolds

Thousands of years
In a time long ago
Our people lived
With more to be told

The Aesir and Vanir
Revered ancestors they be
Remnants of their lives
Lost to history

Conditions for trade
Were well suited
The Aesir-Vanir war
Now concluded

Word had spread
Across the lands
The great war now over
Repairs in demand

A Jotun mason
Couldn't dismiss
The opportunity
Of wealth from this

Traveled he did
With horses and crew
Citadel in rubble
Asgard in view

Presented to Odin
A strong Asgard wall
His plans to rebuild
To protect from all

Odin keenly aware
Of defenses lacked
Needing new walls
Or they'd be attacked

Odin assigned
Loki the task
To negotiate fees
Timeframes to ask

Loki in charge
Of all the details
Didn't consider
All it entails

Loki detested
His role in the plan
Felt it beneath him
To deal with this man

Said to the Jotun
"Get it done quick
Get the wall built
One year the trick"

"I care not the price
Whatever your fee
Asgard will pay
We have gold you see"

The Jotun agreed
To terms laid down
A gleam in his eye
In wealth he'd abound

He set up a pulley
Horse teams in place
Kept them all working
To speed up the pace

His horses were strong
Dutiful and smart
Worked as a unit
Executed their part

Day in and out
And through the nights
Work was constant
Without a blight

Loki took note
The Jotun didn't shirk
His machine with horses
How quickly the work

While building the wall
The Jotun did view
People in Asgard
Norse culture anew

Stunning people
Walking about
Living together
Needing without

Most of them tall
Hair crimson and gold
Eyes green and blue
Bodies so bold

Jealous he was
Of their beauty vast
Lacking in this
He hated their class

He noticed also
Many were smiling
Some holding hands
These people beguiling

Talking of soul mates
The women and men
How to choose one
And how to ascend

As Freyja passed by
Within his gaze
He beheld her beauty
Stunned and amazed

He watched and inspected
She referred to the runes
On her staff engraved
With the sun and the moon

Powerful and enchanted
She commands the sky
Knows when to plant
When it's harvest time

The Jotun decides
Right then and there
His price is Freyja
They must pay this fare

"I'm building their wall"
He thought to himself
"They have so much
I too deserve wealth"

To Loki he called
Announced his fee
"I'll complete the wall
You will give her to me"

Loki in shock
At this turn of events
Afraid to tell Odin
The Jotun's recompense

That very night
Loki lured the steeds
To follow him away
Into the trees

He called and cajoled
And looked all around
Late the next evening
They were finally found

Found all but two
Of his finest horses
No time to search
He must finish the fortress

Demanded of Loki
The Jotun did say
"My work is done
And I want paid"

"I completed your wall
Within the description"
"Pay me now -
Freyja my condition!"

Loki just smiled
Cunning so full
"You're a day late
The contract is null"

The Jotun demanded
With Odin to speak
"I did my part
My prize to reap!"

Odin asked Loki
"Agree to this you did?"
Loki responded
"No! That would be stupid"

In fear of reprisal
Odin would demand
Loki answered and smiled
"I agreed not with this man"

"Liar!" the Jotun cried
"Loki is a cheat
I did my part
He must pay my fee!"

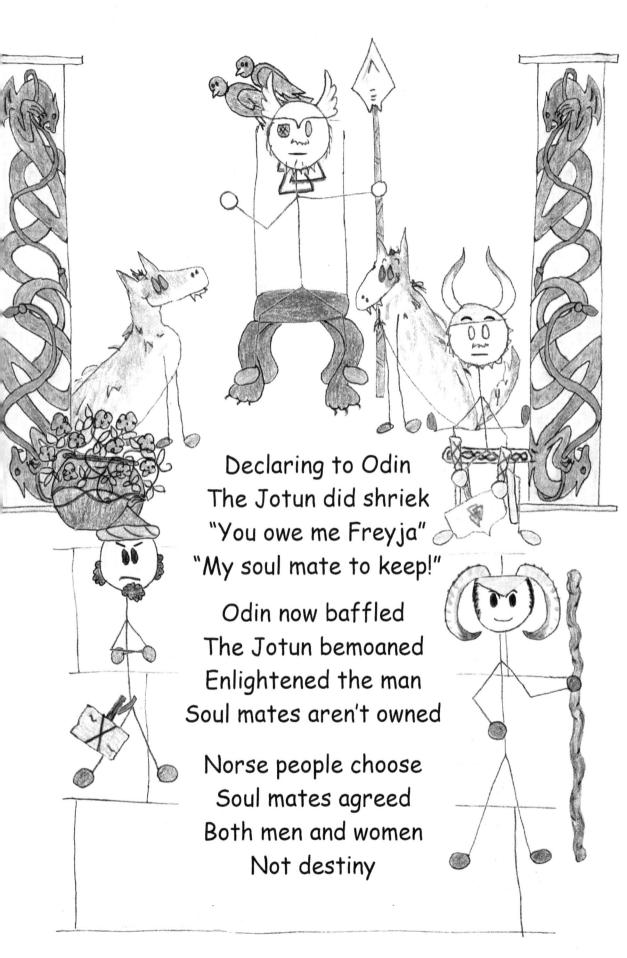

Declaring to Odin
The Jotun did shriek
"You owe me Freyja"
"My soul mate to keep!"

Odin now baffled
The Jotun bemoaned
Enlightened the man
Soul mates aren't owned

Norse people choose
Soul mates agreed
Both men and women
Not destiny

"The contract not done
Within the timeframe
But a wall you did build
I'll pay you the same"

Odin then offered
A fair wealth of gold
For the work that he did
A fortune to hold

The Jotun refused
The offer made
"The sun and the moon
to command I'll be paid"

Odin did further
Attempt to convey
Freyja with her almanac
In Asgard will stay

Explained to the Jotun
Odin did try
Freyja's not a payment
Not for any price

The Jotun continued
To argue and wail
Called Odin names
Asgard assailed

Thor swiftly arose
Offended by such
To call Asgard names
Now that was too much

Raising his hammer
With boundless might
He silenced the Jotun
Without further slight

Then Odin sighed
"Unreasonable man
Just payment offered
That was the plan"

After the ruckus
Did subside
Loki left to retrieve
What he hid outside

Then Loki came forward
Gifts he did bear
Presented to Odin
Covering judgment errored

Beautiful horses
He had in hand
Svadilfare and a mare
Finest in the land

Worked as a team
Eight legs strong
New technology
Asgard has longed

Early next spring
A foal was born
Grey like the clouds
Sleipnir his name to adorn

Odin chose Sleipnir
His bravest steed
Strong and bold
Riding into history

Name Game

Name	Runes
Buri	ᛒᚢᚱᛁ
Freki	ᚠᚱᛖᚲᛁ
Freyja	ᚠᚱᛖᛋᚪ
Freyr	ᚠᚱᛖᚱ
Frigga	ᚠᚱᛁᚷᚷᚪ
Geri	ᚷᛖᚱᛁ
Heimdall	ᚺᛖᛁᛗᛞᚪᛚᛚ
Hugin	ᚺᚢᚷᛁᚾ
Idunna	ᛁᛞᚢᚾᚾᚪ
Kvasir	ᚲᠣᚠᚪᛋᛁᚱ
Loki	ᛚᛟᚲᛁ

Name	Runes
Mimir	ᛗᛁᛗᛁᚱ
Munnin	ᛗᚢᚾᚾᛁᚾ
Njord	ᚾᛋᛟᚱᛞ
Odin	ᛟᛞᛁᚾ
Sif	ᛋᛁᚠ
Sleipnir	ᛋᛚᛖᛁᛈᚾᛁᚱ
Thor	ᚦᛟᚱ
Tyr	ᛏᛁᚱ
Ve	ᚹᛖ
Vili	ᚹᛁᛚᛁ

Find their names in runes on the following pages

Pronunciation Guide

Aesir = [**ay**-sir] said like "ace + sir"

   rhymes with "racer"

Asgard = [**az**-gard] said like "az + guard"

Bergelmir = [**ber**-gil-meer]

   said like "burr + gill + mere"

Bifrost = [**bi**-frost] said like "by + frost"

Buri = [**bur**-ee] rhymes with "blurry"

Edda = [**ed**-uh] rhymes with "data"

Freki = [**fre**-kee] said like "fre + key"

Freyja = [**fray**-yah] said like "fray + ya"

Freyr = [**fray**] said like "fray" rhymes with "say"

Frigga = [**frig**-uh] rhymes with "twig" + "uh"

Geri = [**je**-ree] said like "jerry"

Heimdall = [**hime**-dal] said like "hime + doll"

Hugin = [**hew**-gen] rhymes with "again"

Idunna = [i-**doo**-na] said like "eye + do + na"

Jotun = [**yo**-ten] said like "yo + ten"

Kvasir = [**kvahs**-eer] said like "ka + vas + er"

Loki = [**lo**-kee] said like "low + key"

Mimir = [**mim**-eer] said like "mim + ear"

Munnin = [**mew**-nen] said like "mew + nin"

Njord = [**nee**-yord] said like "knee + y-ord"
rhymes with "cord"

Odin = [**oh**-din] said like "O + den"

Saga = [**sah**-guh] rhymes with "lava"

Seid = [**say**-d] rhymes with "made"

Sif = [**sif**] rhymes with "jif"

Skadi = [skah-**dee**] rhymes with "muddy"

Sleipnir = [**slip**-near] said like "slip + near"

Svadilfare = [**svah**-dill-fare] "svad" rhymes with "gla
said like "svad + dill + fare"

Thor = [**thor**] rhymes with "more"

Tyr = [**teer**] rhymes with "clear"

Vanir = [**vah**-neer] said like "veneer"

Ve = [**vay**] rhymes with "say"

Vili = [**vill**-ee] rhymes with "silly"

Ymir = [**yim**-yeer] said like "yim + year"